W9-BHL-184

Copyright © 1985 by Jomega, Inc./Dreamakers. All rights reserved under International and Pan-American Copyright Conventions. Published in the United States by Random House, Inc., New York, and simultaneously in Canada by Random House of Canada Limited, Toronto.

Library of Congress Cataloging in Publication Data: Cosgrove, Stephen. Gimme. (A Whimsie storybook) SUMMARY: A spell from the Switch Witch turns the gentle Haystack into a greedy creature grabbing everyone else's property. 1. Children's stories, American. [1. Greed—Fiction. 2. Witches—Fiction] I. Reasoner, Charles, ill. II. Title. III. Series: Cosgrove, Stephen. Whimsie storybook. PZ7.C8187Gi 1985 [E] 85-1958 ISBN: 0-394-87451-X

Manufactured in Belgium
1 2 3 4 5 6 7 8 9 0

The Whimsies™ STORYBOOKS

Gimme

by Stephen Cosgrove

illustrated by Charles Reasoner

Random House 🏠 New York

If you looked to the farthest horizon, to the very edge of your fondest wish, you would see the tall, jagged peaks of the Quirk Mountains. Beyond the mountains there flowed a laughing, bubbling stream called the River Whim. And beside this stream, in a meadow of clover and daisies, there was a village of wooden-slat cabins, with wheat-straw roofs and chimneys made from pebbles and sand.

In the village lived furry little creatures called Whimsies. The Whimsies had cute button noses and bright, shiny eyes, and were covered from head to foot with fur as soft as dandelion down.

They worked here. They played here. They slept and they dreamed here. For this was and always would be the home of the Whimsies beside the River Whim, beneath the Quirk Mountains.

Every morning, after the Whimsies ate a hearty breakfast of grains and berries, they walked to the fields at the edge of the meadow to tend their crops.

They worked very hard. Sometimes they would stop to hear a bird sing or to watch a butterfly flutter through the stalks of wheat and corn. Then they would happily go back to their work.

One summer's day Haystack, a little Whimsie with fur as yellow as straw, left his work in the fields to find a shady place to rest. He stretched out in the cool grasses, and before you could count one, two, three, he was fast asleep.

Haystack would have slept there for hours, but suddenly there was a loud snap and crack in the bushes behind him. Haystack woke up and looked about in wide-eyed wonder and loudly asked, "Who is scaring me while I snooze?"

Suddenly Haystack saw an old woman with a laughing little lizard by her side. She patted and primped at her dusty, frizzy hair and said, "Why, hello, little Whimsie! Resting, are we?"

"Yes," said Haystack. "But who are you?"

The old woman looked from side to side, and when she was sure no one was near she answered, "My friends— and I have many—call me Switch Witch, and this is my pet, Wizard Lizard." Her bony hand playfully scratched the scaly head of the giggling lizard.

Haystack stood up and nervously said, "Well, it's been nice meeting you, but I've got to get back to my work."

"Before you go," Switch Witch said in a slippery voice, "would you like to share some of my berries?" She reached into her basket and came up with a handful of plump red berries.

"Mmmm, they certainly look good," Haystack thought. He took a plump, juicy berry and popped it into his mouth.

The berry was sweet, almost too sweet. "What kind of berries are these?" Haystack asked as he reached for another.

"Greed Berries, my little furry friend. You really shouldn't have any more," Switch Witch said slyly.

"GIMME!" demanded Haystack, and he grabbed more and more of the berries.

Switch Witch watched with great delight as Haystack demanded more and more Greed Berries.

When he had gobbled all the berries, Haystack stomped out of the shady glen and headed back to the village. On his way he grabbed an apple off a tree, saying, "Gimme! Gimme! Gimme!"

Like a whirlwind, Haystack charged into the village and saw Woolly Woofer, the Whimsies' only dog, playing with his favorite ball. "I like your ball, Woolly Woofer. So gimme!" said Haystack. And with not so much as a please or a thank you, he grabbed the ball.

For the rest of the day Haystack gimme'd his way throughout the village. He took candy, a bike, and a little doll. "Gimme this!" and "Gimme that!" Haystack grabbed whatever he wanted.

That night the other Whimsies gathered at the old Meeting Hall. Outside, Haystack was still shouting "Gimme!"

"What's come over Haystack?" asked one.

"Switch Witch must have given him some Greed Berries!" said another.

Then Grandma Whimsie, who was the oldest, wisest Whimsie, finally spoke: "There is only one way to break the spell. Haystack must see his own reflection in the still waters of the River Whim. Then he will see his own selfish self, and the power of the Greed Berries will be broken."

Early the next morning all the Whimsies formed a line. It started in the center of the village and wound down the narrow path and over the old, rickety bridge that crossed the River Whim. The first little Whimsie in line held a bright blue ball with yellow stripes.

Soon she saw Haystack coming toward her. "Look! There he is!" she shouted to the others. "Get ready!"

With a glare in his eye and a growl in his voice, Haystack stormed up to her and said, "Gimme that ball!"

The little Whimsie just shook her head. "I can't," she said. "It's not mine." With that she tossed the ball to the next Whimsie.

Haystack was not put off so easily. Down the line he went and to each Whimsie he demanded, "Gimme that ball!"

But each time the Whimsie just shook his head, said it wasn't his ball, and tossed it to the next Whimsie in line.

The ball went from hand to hand. Finally it reached Grandma Whimsie, who was waiting at the Tree of Truth. Haystack said in a very irritated voice, "Gimme that ball! Now!"

Grandma Whimsie smiled and said, "Surely. Here!" And with that she tossed it high up into the tree.

"That isn't going to stop me!" Haystack said as he climbed the tree.

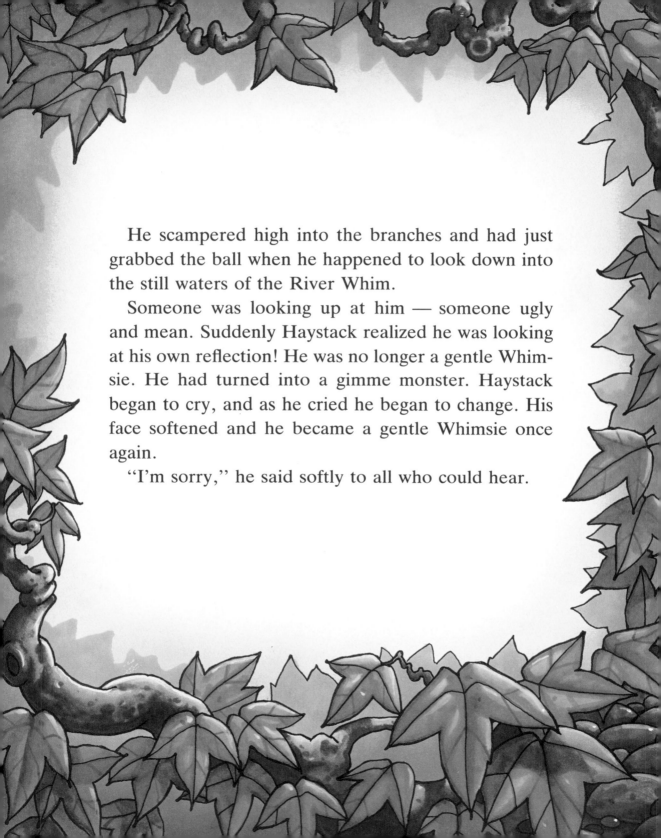

He scampered high into the branches and had just grabbed the ball when he happened to look down into the still waters of the River Whim.

Someone was looking up at him — someone ugly and mean. Suddenly Haystack realized he was looking at his own reflection! He was no longer a gentle Whimsie. He had turned into a gimme monster. Haystack began to cry, and as he cried he began to change. His face softened and he became a gentle Whimsie once again.

"I'm sorry," he said softly to all who could hear.

Switch Witch angrily watched all this from behind the tall weeds that grew at the edge of the river. Unfortunately Wizard Lizard, who was a little hungry, reached into Switch Witch's basket and snitched a Greed Berry. Did he stop at just one? No, of course not. He took another and another and another.

Switch Witch tried to dash into the forest, but a greedy Wizard Lizard was close behind her shouting "Gimme! Gimme! Gimme!" all the way.

As for Haystack, he returned to the fields and the work that he loved. If and when he wanted to borrow something that did not belong to him, Haystack would always ask with a please and accept with a thank you.

If you wish
to take from others
Those things not your own,
Remember a whimsie
called Haystack
And the lesson
he was shown.